MOMMA <u>WOULD</u> COME BACK!

"She's not dead. She's coming home."
Jenny begged Daddy to understand.
She sat small and defenseless in the
high-backed chair.

But Sara knew Momma wasn't coming
home. Momma had died in the railway accident far away in Switzerland,
where she had gone for a short winter
holiday with her cousins. Sara and
Jenny had watched the suitcases being
packed for the trip; exchanged with
Momma last kisses and hugs; promised
to be good girls. At the last minute
Jenny began to cry. Momma hugged
her close. "I love you, Jenny-wren. I'll
be home soon."

REMEMBER ME WHEN I AM DEAD

Carol Beach York

BANTAM BOOKS
TORONTO · NEW YORK · LONDON · SYDNEY

No character in this book is intended to
represent any actual person; all the
incidents of the story are entirely
fictional in nature.

*This low-priced Bantam Book
has been completely reset in a type face
designed for easy reading, and was printed
from new plates. It contains the complete
text of the original hard-cover edition.*
NOT ONE WORD HAS BEEN OMITTED.

RL 4, IL age 11 and up

REMEMBER ME WHEN I AM DEAD
*A Bantam Book / published by arrangement with
Thomas Nelson Inc.*

PRINTING HISTORY
*Thomas Nelson edition published May 1980
Bantam edition / September 1981*

ISBN 0-553-20213-8

Published simultaneously in the United States and Canada

for
Rose Cantwell
an elegant lady

REMEMBER ME
WHEN I AM
DEAD

The room was dark except for a small circle of lamplight on the desk.

The only sound was the soft movement of a pencil across the inside cover of a book lying open in the lamplight.

> Roses are blue
> Violets are red
> Remember me
> When I am dead
>   Momma

The words were written slowly, carefully, in a round childish hand.

There was the faint breath of a sigh, and the book closed silently. The pencil, laid upon the desk, rolled a few inches and came to a stop against the base of the lamp.

The lamp switch clicked off, and the room was dark.

1

The Loring house was a mile out of town. The road wound through winter woods under a cloud-cast sky, and the only spot of color in this landscape of bare branches and white snow on frozen ground was a yellow school bus making its homeward trip.

Most of the children had already been let off, and the scanty group of remaining children sang "Jingle Bells" in piping voices as the trees sped by the windows and school days were left behind for two wonderful weeks of Christmas vacation.

The bus stopped at the Loring driveway to let off one small girl, who was in too much of a hurry to answer the driver's last cheery call: "Merry Christmas!"

As the bus drove off along the wintry road edged with snow and leafless trees, Jenny Loring raced up the driveway and along the side of the house toward the kitchen door. Her face was bright with excitement. Dark hair streamed below a red knit cap with a pompon.

Overhead the graceful shade trees of summer stood starkly bare against the graying December sky. In the summer peony bushes bloomed along the driveway, but the summer flowers were gone and all the warm golden light of summer days.

Smoke rose from the chimney of the house and blew away into the wind.

Indoors, lamps were already lighted; winter afternoons were short.

Jenny burst into the kitchen with such a rush that Mrs. Dow, neatly trimming a pie crust, looked up with surprise—but Jenny flew right by her. "Where's Daddy?"

Before Mrs. Dow could answer, Jenny was gone, running through the kitchen and along the polished hall floor toward the living room.

"He might be almost anywhere." Mrs. Dow continued the conversation to an empty room. She was a tall, large-boned woman with a bun of gray hair at the back of her head. She nodded to herself as she spoke, trimming expertly at the pie crust. "He might be in his study. Or he might be upstairs."

4

She thought a bit.

"Maybe he's in the living room. Yes, that's probably where he is, I would think."

Mrs. Dow was used to Jenny. Jenny came and went like a bird on the wing, living in a place Mrs. Dow could only faintly recall: childhood. A land of enchantment from which Mrs. Dow had long ago departed.

But Mr. Loring wasn't in the living room. Only Margaret and Sara were there, sorting through Christmas ornaments they had brought down from the upstairs storage closet.

The room was strewn with boxes of fragile colored balls. A flimsy cardboard package of icicles lay on the seat of a chair, spilling silvery strands upon the cushion.

Margaret had untangled a string of Christmas lights and was testing them just as Jenny came running to the door. The bulbs lighted up in a blaze of red and green and blue and yellow, just as Jenny popped in—and she stopped short for a moment, taking in this glorious sight of lights and ornaments and boxes.

Margaret looked up with a smile. She

was a pretty woman with soft yellow hair
and gray-blue eyes, and she was happy to be
getting out Christmas things on this cold
December afternoon in the firelight and
lamplight. All the happiness of this was on
her face. And now Jenny was home to join
in.

"Jenny—"

But Jenny ran across the room, where
Sara knelt beside a large box, drawing out
another string of lights. Sara, who was thin
and quiet, was tall for her age, and she
never rushed into rooms glowing with
news.

"Sara—I saw Mr. Hoffman!"

Sara looked up from the box with surprise. Her solemn dark eyes rested on
Jenny's excited face. "You *did?* Where?"

"By school. I was on the bus, and I
pounded on the window, but he didn't see
me."

Ordinarily Sara would have been on
the school bus herself. But she was getting
over a cold, so she had missed this last day
of school before the Christmas holidays.

"Where's Daddy—I want to tell
Daddy." Jenny spun around toward Margaret, who knelt on the floor beside the

6

gleaming strand of lights casting their colors upon the carpet.

"He's in his study." Margaret's smile of curiosity invited Jenny to tell her who Mr. Hoffman was and why seeing him was so special. But again, as with Mrs. Dow, Jenny vanished. Through the doorway Margaret could see her dashing along the hall, the pompon on her cap bobbing crazily.

"Who on earth is Mr. Hoffman?" Margaret unplugged the lights and drew the string aside to a safe place along the edge of the carpet.

"Oh . . ." Sara hesitated. "He's an old man we used to know. He was a friend of Momma."

She pretended to be busy taking strings of Christmas lights from the box. She thought maybe Daddy's new wife wouldn't want to hear about friends of Momma.

"You sounded surprised when Jenny said she saw him." Margaret still didn't understand what all the commotion was about. Her gray-blue eyes were gentle, questioning.

Sara fiddled with the Christmas lights. Dark hair drooped around her face.

"He went away. He wasn't ever coming back."

The conversation fell off.

Silence hung heavily in the room.

Margaret felt a dull foreboding that even the bright Christmas decorations could not dispel.

She was so newly married—only a month. She was Jenny and Sara's new mother, yet she so often felt the presence of their real mother hovering close in the rooms of the house, waiting like an eerie shadow to darken unexpected moments, a returning spirit of memory that would not surrender.

2

ஐ Margaret didn't know whether or not to ask any more questions about Mr. Hoffman. To fill the awkward silence she said, "I think I need a good hot cup of coffee."

She left the Christmas lights and went to the windows, drawing the heavy silk draperies partly closed. The draperies were green, flecked with gold thread. They rustled softly as Margaret pulled the cord. By and by the Christmas tree would stand here at the windows, and a hundred tiny Christmas lights would shine out into the darkness.

A chair and table by the windows would have to be moved aside to make room for the tree. Margaret lingered a moment, measuring the space with her eyes. But she was uncomfortably aware of Sara behind her in the silent room.

"He was this nice old German man,"

Sara said softly. "He lived in a little house in the woods."

Margaret turned. Sara was still kneeling by the large Christmas box, her face hidden by long dark hair.

"He carved things. One time he made me a little bird to hang on the Christmas tree. It's probably here somewhere." Sara kept her eyes down. She was unwinding a string of Christmas lights, and her fingers trembled as she remembered the little bird . . . and Mr. Hoffman's little house in the woods . . . and Momma.

"When did he go away?"

For a moment Margaret thought Sara wasn't going to answer. Firelight flickered on the hearth tiles, gleamed on the brass log bucket. A vase reflected on the smooth, dark surface of a table. Around the room empty chairs with open arms seemed to be listening, waiting.

"The last time I saw him was at Momma's funeral."

Margaret didn't know what to say to that.

Daylight was fading at the windows. A lusterless winter twilight was creeping over the woods.

10

"Aren't you going to get your coffee?" Sara's voice was strained.

"Yes, I think I will."

Margaret tried to sound cheerful, as though she didn't notice Sara was close to tears. She went to the living-room doorway, stepping carefully around the Christmas things. Out of the corner of her eye she could see Sara's bent head. But how could she comfort Sara even if she stayed? Margaret wondered; she was actually glad to escape from the room. Suddenly she was tired looking through Christmas boxes. Suddenly everything had changed.

Alone in the living room, Sara pushed aside the box of lights and began to poke around in the other boxes. Now that she remembered Mr. Hoffman's bird, she wanted to find it. It was painted red and hung on a red velvet ribbon. Momma had fixed the ribbon.

When Sara put it on the tree each Christmas, the bird bobbed and swayed as if it were flying.

Sara was surprised to feel tears stinging her eyes as she looked through the first box and then a second box and didn't find the bird. What if it was lost and she never found it again?

She had been crying the last time she ever saw Mr. Hoffman. In this very room. He sat on a small beige-cushioned chair, looking awkward and out of place in his worn brown suit, holding a delicate coffee cup in his gnarled hands.

The room that was so silent now had been filled with the murmur of voices.

It had been winter then, too. Mid-January; cold and bleak with a melancholy late-afternoon light outside, much as it was now.

Sara sat on a chair by Mr. Hoffman, feeling lost and forlorn among the relatives and friends who had come to the house after the funeral services. The two of them, sitting at the side of the room, were somewhat withdrawn from the others, who clustered on the sofas by the fireplace and moved back and forth through the hall to the dining room. Mrs. Dow had set out cake and sandwiches on the dining-room table. Aunt Irene, looking pale in a black dress, poured coffee from Momma's silver service.

It was like a party in a bad dream.

Sara's face had been swollen and red

from crying, and even then, after the funeral, tears kept coming into her eyes. But Jenny didn't cry at all, and Jenny was the little one.

"Why can't I be brave like Jenny?" Tears glistened on Sara's cheeks.

Mr. Hoffman gazed down at her mournfully. His eyes were almost lost below bushy white brows. His face had a thousand lines.

"It is better to cry," he said gently.

"No, it's not." Sara brushed at her tears. But Mr. Hoffman nodded his head and said yes, it was better to cry.

And he had been right. Jenny never did cry, and afterward Sara heard everybody say that was wrong. Aunt Irene for one. Sara had lots of times heard Aunt Irene telling Daddy it would be better if Jenny cried. "More normal," Aunt Irene said. Furrows of worry creased her forehead. To think of Jenny not crying. . . . "It isn't good to keep such a deep grief bottled up inside."

It was all true. Sara cried, a big girl nearly thirteen years old. But by and by she stopped crying. By and by she got used to

13

Momma's being gone. But Jenny had all the dreams about Momma.

"She's not dead! She's not dead!" Jenny had insisted, dry-eyed, shrill, bewildered. She dodged away whenever Daddy or Aunt Irene held out their arms to comfort her. She put her fingers in her ears if anyone said they were sorry her Momma died. A boy at school asked Jenny what happened to her Momma, and Jenny kicked him in the shins. "She just doesn't understand, poor darling," Aunt Irene told Daddy. Finally, as the weeks went by, Daddy wouldn't talk about it anymore. Nobody talked about it. And Jenny had dreams about Momma.

"I had a dream about Momma last night," she would confide at the breakfast table.

"What was it?" Sara would ask curiously, darting a glance at Daddy who would frown and look unhappy. The morning newspaper always lay by his place; his spoon jangled as he stirred cream into his coffee.

"She was walking in the snow, in the mountains, like the postcard she sent."

Or another time: "We had a party at school, and Momma came and we had cake.

Teacher said Momma couldn't have any cake, but Momma just laughed."

"Jenny." Daddy looked distressed and helpless.

"She's not dead. She's coming home." Jenny begged Daddy to understand. She sat small and defenseless in the high-backed chair. Under the table her feet didn't even reach the floor.

But Sara knew Momma wasn't coming home. Momma had died in the railway accident far away in Switzerland, where she had gone for a short winter holiday with her cousins. Daddy couldn't go because of business. Sara and Jenny watched the suitcases being packed for the trip; exchanged with Momma last kisses and hugs; promised to be good girls, do their homework, mind Mrs. Dow. At the last minute Jenny began to cry. Momma hugged her close. "I love you, Jenny-wren. I'll be home soon."

Momma had died in an instant. Maybe if she had been sick for a while first, like some people were, Jenny might have understood better. But Momma was just suddenly gone. Sara understood. She cried and

15

missed Momma, but she didn't dream about her coming home again.

Aunt Irene thought Jenny should go away to school.

"She needs a change of scene," Aunt Irene said. "She needs to get away from this house. There are too many memories of her mother here. New places bring new thoughts and new experiences. That's what Jenny needs."

But nothing came of it. Daddy thought Jenny was too little to be sent away to school.

After what seemed a long time, Jenny stopped having dreams. Everybody said everything would be all right now.

And then Margaret began coming to dinner, and afternoon drives, and summer picnics. The peonies bloomed along the driveway and robins hopped on the lawn, digging their beaks into the grass to catch worms. The days were long and warm and full of sunlight. Margaret played with Jenny and made her laugh. Aunt Irene said it would be good for Jenny and Sara to have a woman in the house again—which was not counting Mrs. Dow, of course. Mrs. Dow was the housekeeper, and she already had a husband, so she couldn't be their new mother.

"What will we call her?" Sara asked when Daddy said he was going to marry Margaret. It was important to Sara to get that straightened out.

Jenny twisted a strand of hair and waited for Daddy to answer. She seemed to understand that she was going to have a new mother, and she drew close to Daddy to share her feelings.

"I like her." Jenny's voice was soft, barely a whisper.

Daddy laughed. "I'm glad you like her." He gathered Jenny into his lap and held her close.

Sara stood by the chair.

"What are we going to call her?" she asked again. That was the important thing.

They finally decided on "Margaret." Which was right. It wouldn't have been right to call her "Momma." Momma was dead.

Sara found the little carved bird at last. The velvet ribbon was nearly as fresh as ever, although Sara had been only six or seven when Mr. Hoffman gave her the carving.

She lifted the bird from the box of Christmas ornaments and swung the ribbon. The bird bobbed and swirled as if it were really flying. . . . Sara wondered if seeing Mr. Hoffman would start Jenny talking about Momma and having dreams again.

3

∾ Sara wasn't the only one who
wondered if Mr. Hoffman would bring back
with him too many old memories.

Sara's father wondered too.

Mr. Loring was trying to make a new
life for himself, and for Sara and Jenny. It
was a great joy to him that Sara and Jenny
accepted their stepmother so well and
seemed to be happy.

And Margaret was good to the girls.
There had been many happy times these
past months. Mr. Loring wanted them to
continue. He was, on this cold December
day, rather sorry to hear that Jenny had
seen Mr. Hoffman, but it could not be
helped.

Jenny had not been gone from the
study long before Margaret came, bringing
the tray of coffee Mr. Loring liked on afternoons when he was home from the office
early.

Margaret sat down companionably in

the armchair by his desk and leaned her head back with an air of restfulness, content to be here in the room she liked best in all the house.

The reddish brown of the mahogany desk was matched by the dark amber-colored carpet. The walls were lined with books, and the bay window gave a wide view of the back garden and the woods in the distance. The high-backed wing chairs made Margaret think of old-fashioned inn rooms where distinguished gentlemen might sit to smoke their pipes and enjoy a glass of brandy after dinner. When she sat in the room, Margaret could imagine the nearby sound of carriage wheels on a foggy London street.

Perhaps the room was her favorite because it was so much Charles's room. Margaret didn't sense lingering memories of Evelyn Loring in this room, as she did in other parts of the house. The room held her close, warm, protected . . . now why had she thought of protection? she wondered. There was nothing she needed protection from.

Mr. Loring stirred cream into his

coffee and brooded at the cup as though it might reveal some secret to him.

"Charles?"

He looked up to find Margaret regarding him fondly.

"What are you looking so serious about?"

He made a small gesture. "It's nothing really—did Jenny tell you?"

"That she saw Mr. Hoffman? Yes, she did. She was in a great hurry to tell you."

Mr. Loring smiled faintly, recalling how Jenny had rushed in. "I suppose you wonder who he is."

"Sara said he was an old friend of Evelyn," Margaret answered calmly, with just the right mixture of interest and nonchalance. She had not expected to marry a widower and never hear about old friends, old times.

Mr. Loring sipped his coffee absently. Light from the large bronze desk lamp cast a sheen on his dark hair, glinted on the heavy gold ring he wore on one finger. He was a handsome man, with fine features and a look of distinction and success. But now, with his tie loosened, shirt cuffs turned back, a shadow of sadness in his eyes, he looked tired, vulnerable, and Margaret longed to comfort him in some way. She loved him very much.

"Sara said Mr. Hoffman wasn't ever coming back."

Mr. Loring shook his head. "We didn't think he would. Funny old guy."

"Why did he go away?"

Mr. Loring shrugged. "He always said he would go back to Germany someday. The winters here were too severe for him. He had a cottage in the woods near the skating pond—old, drafty place, no way to keep it really warm. Evelyn said she had to keep her coat on when she visited him on cold days. Wind rattled the windows and came in everywhere. Finally last winter he left and went back to the town in Germany where he grew up. He had a sister living there. I thought it was a good decision on his part."

"Why would he come back?" Margaret was puzzled.

"I can't imagine." Mr. Loring shook his head again. "Whatever the reason, I'm rather sorry about it. Evelyn had sort of befriended him—you know, lonely old man in his poor little house. She used to take Jenny and Sara to visit him. He was a kindly old fellow, and the girls loved to go to see him. He told them stories about his boyhood in Germany, made them cocoa, things like that. I just hope having him back won't stir up too many memories."

He didn't say "for Jenny," but they both knew that was what he meant. It would be too bad. Jenny had been so much better these past months.

Outside the afternoon had darkened. Lamplight was intensified in the growing gloom of twilight.

"Perhaps it won't be so bad." Margaret patted her husband's hand. "The girls are busy with school and things. They'll probably hardly see him."

"They'll see him tomorrow, I'm afraid," Mr. Loring said regretfully. "Jenny made me promise to stop by his house when we go for the Christmas tree."

He looked at Margaret apologetically.

"We'll be going right by his house, and Jenny wanted to see him so much I couldn't say no."

He had never been able to say no to Jenny.

23

Evelyn had never been able to say no to Jenny.

No one could say no to that expectant pixie face and pleading eyes.

He supposed he and Evelyn had spoiled Jenny over the years. They wanted to give her everything; he still did.

"Please, can we stop and see Mr. Hoffman tomorrow?"

Jenny had stood close beside his study chair, leaning gently on his arm, looking up into his eyes.

Her small fingers plucked his sleeve hopefully.

He couldn't say no.

There wasn't any logical reason to say no. They would be driving right by the cottage in the woods.

If Mr. Hoffman was there, with reminders of bygone times wrapping him like a mournful cloak, they would have to face it sooner or later.

4

A light snow fell during the night, etching the tree branches as though a feathery brush had been drawn across each bough. The air was crisp and clear and still after the snowfall. A bright winter sun rose over the road and the woods and the snowy land. It was a perfect day to get a Christmas tree.

"Can we get the biggest tree in the whole woods?" Jenny wanted to know.

She stood in the back of the car, leaning close to Daddy's face, breathing soft breaths upon his cheek.

Every year since Jenny and Sara could remember, Daddy had taken them to Crosby's Tree Farm. At Crosby's you didn't just buy a Christmas tree—you went walking around among the trees and chose the very one you wanted and chopped it down yourself.

The pond, nearly frozen over now, was

on the outskirts of town. Although it seemed a long walk to Jenny and Sara when they went skating there, it appeared in view in moments when they were driving in the car.

"There's the pond," Jenny announced, pointing a mitten toward the woods. "Sara fell in one time."

"She did?" Margaret looked at the pond and then turned her head to smile at Sara in the back seat. "I bet that was fun."

Sara made a face.

"She sure did," Mr. Loring said. He was looking at Sara in the rear-view mirror. Sara wished everybody would stop looking at her and talking about how she fell through the ice. It was a long time ago. She still hated the pond—but no one knew. No one knew she was afraid to skate there. It was her secret.

Then almost at once they had passed the pond, and Jenny was saying, "There's Mr. Hoffman's house," pointing again with a mittened hand.

Mr. Loring sighed under his breath as he turned the car from the main road onto a narrow dirt road that led back through the trees a short distance and came to an end in front of a small house with six rickety wooden steps leading to a scrap of porch.

He stopped the car and sat for a moment staring at the cottage with surprise.

There was a deserted, closed-up look about the small frame house under the snowy trees. No footprints broke the freshly fallen snow upon the steps and porch. The windows were bare, each sill lined with snow below uncurtained frames of glass. Surely no one was living here.

Jenny had thrown open the back door of the car and hopped out.

"Come on, Sara—" She tugged at her sister's sleeve. "Won't Mr. Hoffman be surprised to see us!"

Sara scrambled out after Jenny. A long green muffler trailed tassels down her back. They ran up the steps together and pounded on the front door, as Mr. Loring and Margaret got out of the car and stood gazing uncertainly at the forlorn, abandoned house.

There was no answer to the knocks on the door. A bird twittered somewhere far off, but otherwise the woods lay in silence around them. Margaret drew up her coat collar around her face, shivering in the cold.

Sara gave up knocking and went along the porch to peer in through a window. Jenny banged on the door again and called, "Mr. Hoffman—Mr. Hoffman—it's me."

Margaret came up the porch steps and stood behind Sara at the window—through which they could dimly see a small, unfurnished room. Margaret turned with a puzzled expression as her husband joined her on the porch.

"Charles, I don't think there's anyone here."

Mr. Loring shaded his eyes and looked through the window. The room inside was completely empty, unused. No one was living there now or had for a long time. He exchanged a questioning look with Margaret, and though no word was spoken, they thought they knew what had really happened: Jenny had been thinking about her Momma again and then she imagined she saw Mr. Hoffman . . . friend of Momma. All the trouble of the past year lay around them fresh and hurting and sad again.

Jenny tugged at her father's coat. "Why doesn't he open the door, Daddy?"

"He's not here," Sara turned from the window with disappointment. "I thought you saw him. I thought he was back."

"He *is*," Jenny insisted loudly.

"I'm afraid no one's here, Jenny," her father said gently.

"But he has to be. I saw him."

"Maybe it was just someone who looked like Mr. Hoffman," Margaret suggested. Jenny's face startled her, it had suddenly become so tense and troubled below the little red knit cap.

"It wasn't. It was Mr. Hoffman. I saw him." Jenny's voice rose shrilly. "He's here."

It was the same defiant, frustrated way in which she had insisted that Momma wasn't really dead.

Sara looked at Daddy—who was reaching out just a fraction too late for his hand to catch hold of Jenny as she darted off.

"Maybe he's around in back. I'll go find him."

Jenny ran down the steps and around the side of the house toward the back.

"She made it up." Sara felt disappointed. It would have been so good to see Mr. Hoffman again. He had always loved her. He had carved her little bird. She turned and pressed her face close to the glass hopelessly, seeing in memory the bare room furnished with Mr. Hoffman's chairs, the table by the fire, the footstool where she liked to sit, hugging her knees and listening to his stories. Momma sat on the threadbare couch, drawing off gloves and rubbing her fingers slowly so Mr. Hoffman wouldn't notice she was cold. A hundred afternoons of memory flooded over Sara. Fire glowed in the little fireplace, cocoa heated on the stove. . . . Mr. Hoffman was opening the package Momma brought, for they never came empty-handed.

"Ah, what do we have here?" Mr. Hoffman's kindly blue eyes, hooded by gray brows, gleamed with appropriate pleasure —and Jenny would hop from one foot to another telling him, as though he could not see for himself, "It's cake, Mr. Hoffman."

He would nod happily. "Well, then, we must all have a piece."

"Oh, no." Momma would hold up a protesting hand, small and fragile—so unlike Mr. Hoffman's hands, which were broad and old, and covered with curling black hairs, "No, Mr. Hoffman, it's for you."

"I can't eat alone," he would protest.

Sara and Jenny would run to get plates from the cupboard. They had known all along they would be invited to have some cake.

Momma would shake her head, smiling. "Mr. Hoffman, Mr. Hoffman," she scolded. She worried that he didn't have enough to eat. Besides the cake, there was sometimes sausage and cheese, or a fresh loaf of Mrs. Dow's bread.

When the cake was eaten, while Sara and Jenny lingered over their cocoa, Mr. Hoffman would light his pipe. It had a sweet smell, like dried apples and smoky autumn leaves. Then he would tell them stories about Germany.

"When I was a boy ..."

All this Sara saw in the empty room, nearly so dark she could not even actually make out the shape of the cold hearth where so many bright fires had once burned. Behind her, Margaret was saying, "Maybe it's me, Charles—having a new mother, so to speak. Or maybe it's the holidays. The first Christmas without her mother."

Margaret rested her hands lightly on Sara's shoulders and sighed unhappily. Jenny was imagining again—imagining she had seen Mr. Hoffman, that he was back, and that somehow, because of this first step, everything would go back to the way it was before.

"My sister thought Jenny should go away to school, and perhaps she was right," Mr. Loring mused.

He stared off into the woods and shook his head with a puzzled air.

"I thought Jenny would miss her friends. I didn't know how she would get along away from the only home she's ever known. It seemed wrong to uproot her and send her away."

Margaret listened sympathetically. Everything Charles said sounded right to her. Jenny was too little to send away from home.

From far off behind the cottage they could hear Jenny's voice, tremulous in the cold winter morning:

"Mr. Hoffman—Mr. Hoffman—where are you?"

Margaret drew her collar closer. But there was no way to get warm, no way to shut out Jenny's voice. There was an aura of desolation about the lonesome house, a haunting sound to the small voice calling "Mr. Hoffman—Mr. Hoffman—where are you?"

"Jenny seemed to be getting along so well, I forgot about the whole idea of sending her away to school." Mr. Loring turned toward Margaret. "But perhaps we should consider it again."

"Perhaps," Margaret answered uncertainly. She wasn't sure what was right to do.

Sara thought about Jenny going away to school. She looked up at Margaret's face, but there was no answer there one way or another. Sara thought of this school, wherever it was, as a mean place with strict teachers and hard rules. Jenny would be alone and far from home.

"Are you cold?" Margaret felt Sara shivering, and without stopping to think that Sara was quite a big girl now, she tightened the green muffler with a motherly gesture.

"We're all cold standing here." Mr. Loring's own uncertainty and disappointment about the whole situation brought an edge of impatience to his voice. He went down the porch stairs and walked to the side of the house. "Come on, Jenny. Time to go."

Jenny appeared, her hair falling in her eyes, her cheeks red with cold. "I haven't found Mr. Hoffman yet," she begged. "Maybe he's in the woods somewhere."

"No he's not, Jenny. He's not here."

"But, Daddy—"

"It's too cold to stand here arguing, Jenny. Get into the car, and we'll get the tree."

"Yes, we'll get the tree." Margaret held out her hand to Jenny and tried to make her think of happier things.

"I want to see Mr. Hoffman." Jenny pulled back reluctantly, but Margaret took her hand and started toward the car, saying, "I want to see this marvelous place where you chop down your own Christmas tree."

Margaret's cheerful manner did no good. Jenny sat in the back seat of the car pouting silently at the passing countryside. Sara sat far away on the opposite end of the seat and looked out of her window, and no one said anything more as they drove along.

5

It was that night, just after Jenny and Sara had gone up to get ready for bed, that Margaret found the book.

It was Jenny's geography book, left lying on the floor at the edge of the fireplace in the living room.

Margaret picked it up and casually ruffled the pages, seeing the bright schoolbook pictures of nomad tribes and Chinese temples slip by. Then, as she was going to close the book, she caught sight of the verse written on the inside front cover.

> *Roses are blue*
> *Violets are red*
> *Remember me*
> *When I am dead*
> > *Momma*

Margaret felt a chill sweep through her body as she read the verse over again.

Remember me when I am dead. The color drained from her face, and she held the book out to her husband. "Charles, look at this. . . ."

Mr. Loring was prodding the logs with a poker. He turned and glanced at the book absently.

"It's one of Jenny's schoolbooks." Margaret held out the book with the cover open. In a round childish hand the name "Jennifer Loring, Room 102" was written across the top. Halfway down was the verse.

> *Roses are blue*
> *Violets are red*
> *Remember me*
> *When I am dead*
> *Momma*

"What would make her write such a thing?" Mr. Loring sank into a chair by the fireplace and gazed at the words.

Margaret didn't know. She pressed her lips together and shook her head. "It's a geography book," she said after a moment. "Maybe there's something about Switzerland and it made Jenny think about her mother—oh, I don't know, Charles. Such a grim little verse." Margaret's voice faded off.

By the windows the Christmas tree stood in its stand. The next day, when the boughs had come down a bit from the warmth of the room, it would be time to put on the lights and ornaments and Mr. Hoffman's red bird on the red velvet ribbon.

"I think we should talk to her," Mr. Loring said. He didn't sound really sure. He sounded tired and defeated.

"Oh, Charles—what can we say?" Margaret regarded him across the flickering firelight. They had both been so sure everything was going to be all right. It had been autumn. "Marry me," Charles had said. And Margaret loved him so very much.

"What about the girls?" she had asked. Sunlight was golden around them. The leaves on the trees were red, blazing in the sunlight, rustling on the path through the woods where they walked. The whole world was beautiful that October day.

"The girls like you," he promised. "They need you. I need you."

"Are you sure it isn't too soon?"

"No," he said. "No, it's not too soon."

But it *had* been too soon. Margaret felt sorrow and regret. Jenny was still thinking about her Momma. She didn't want a new mother. She didn't want Margaret....

"Charles?" Margaret asked again. He hadn't answered her. "What can we say?"

Mr. Loring sighed. "We can't just let her go on like this."

Margaret knew he was right. Little girls, dear little girls like Jenny, should have their minds full of happy things. Baking cookies. Putting together jigsaw puzzles. Waiting for Santa Claus to come on Christmas Eve. How old was Jenny? Only nine. Santa Claus was coming to fill her Christmas stocking with candy and oranges. Margaret wanted her to be happy now and forever.

Mr. Loring went to the foot of the stairs and called to Jenny, who came down in a pair of pink-checked pajamas. She had just washed her face, and strands of damp hair stuck to her forehead. Margaret wanted to hug her and tell her how much she loved her. But she held back. It was up to Jenny's father to decide what to do.

Jenny took the book and knelt by the

firelight to read. Margaret sat twisting her fingers unhappily.

> *Roses are blue*
> *Violets are red*
> *Remember me*
> *When I am dead*
> *Momma*

"Jenny." Mr. Loring's voice was husky. She left the book on the hearth and came to the circle of his outstretched arm.

"Why did you write that, sweetheart?"

"I didn't write it." Jenny's voice wavered. "Momma wrote it."

Mr. Loring glanced at Margaret for help. Outside, a few flakes of winter snow drifted toward the room from the darkness of the night, melting upon the windowpane. A log in the fireplace shifted and sent up a small shower of sparks.

"Jenny, Momma's gone. You've got to understand that."

"But, Daddy—"

He put a finger lightly on her lips. "Jenny, Momma's not coming back. Mr. Hoffman isn't back, and Momma's not coming back. She didn't write in your book."

Jenny hung her head. A tear slid down her cheek.

"Open that drawer." Mr. Loring motioned toward the table by his chair.

Jenny turned uncertainly. The drawer slid open with a faint sound of contents shifting inside.

"Is there a pencil there?"

Jenny nodded, brushing at her tears. Her face felt wet and sticky, and more tears welled up into her eyes.

"Bring me the book," Mr. Loring said. "Now erase the verse, Jenny."

Jenny stood at the table, scrubbing away at the words with the pencil eraser. Her hands were so tiny, Margaret thought sadly—thin little-girl fingers cramped around the pencil. When she was done, the words still gleamed palely upon the page. They could never be entirely rubbed away. *Roses are blue . . . Violets are red. . . .* The words would always be there, dim as ghosts.

The stairs had never seemed so long to Jenny. She saw them through a blur of tears, stretching up and far away above her. Her room was lonely, shadowy; she got into bed and pulled the covers over her head, burying her face in the pillow. Oh, if only Momma would come to kiss her good-night like she used to, and read her a story. "Once upon a time there was a beautiful princess..."

"What did Daddy want?" Sara's voice came from the doorway.

Jenny pushed the covers from her face. Sara stood silhouetted in the light from the hall.

"Why are you crying?"

Jenny sniffed back her tears. "Momma wrote me a poem."

Sara came a few steps into the room. "How could Momma write you a poem?"

"She did," Jenny insisted. "Daddy made me erase it."

Sara didn't answer. Snowflakes touched the windows softly in the darkness. There was not a sound in all the house. Light from the hall gave an eerie radiance to the room, casting shadows on the walls.

"Go to sleep," Sara said at last. She came toward the bed in the dim, shadowy light. "Everything will be all right." She tucked the covers around Jenny, like Momma used to do, but Jenny pushed them away and tried to sit up.

42

"Can I sleep with you tonight?"

Sara didn't mind. "Sure, if you want to."

Jenny slipped out from the covers and padded after Sara in her bare feet. She didn't want to sleep alone in the dark room where Momma never came anymore to read stories.

That night Jenny dreamed about Mr. Hoffman. He was standing in a misty place that had no ground or sky, no beginning or end.

He held out his hand to her. He was smiling.

He was going to take her to Momma. She ran toward him through swirls of white mist that were like clouds in heaven.

Mr. Hoffman held out his hand.

6

By Sunday evening the tree was trimmed. The lights, strung first on the fragrant green boughs, began to reflect and sparkle in the shiny globes of the fragile ornaments, on the loops of tinsel flecked with gold, the shimmering silvery icicles—until all the tree was glowing with light and color.

Sara worked solemnly, for it was an important occasion, trimming the Christmas tree. She hung Mr. Hoffman's little bird in a prominent place on the front of the tree, just at her own eye level; as ornaments were put on, she kept stepping back to see how the tree looked.

Margaret thought Jenny seemed happy, trimming the tree. Nothing more was said about the verse written in the book. Maybe everything would be all right after all.

But Margaret's hopes were short-lived.

The next morning, shortly after Mr. Loring had left for the office, Mrs. Dow came into the living room carrying a white envelope. Margaret was sewing a button on one of Jenny's blouses. She was sitting by the windows, glancing out occasionally to watch Sara and Jenny trying to build a snowman in the front yard. The snow was too powdery to pack well, and the snowman was more a misshapen heap than a true snowman.

"Is the mail here already?" Margaret was surprised to see Mrs. Dow bringing the envelope. The mail rarely came before noon.

"Not yet." Mrs. Dow's expression was grave. "I found this on the hall table with the letters to go out. Mr. Loring forgot to take them this morning."

She handed the envelope to Margaret with a reluctant gesture. It was addressed in round, childish writing:

> *Mrs. Loring*
> *Clarion Hotel*
> *Switzerland*

There was no stamp.

Margaret gazed at the address with

confusion. "Where did you say you found this?"

"On the hall table. I just now noticed it on top of the others. She's written to her mother, poor little thing." Mrs. Dow folded her hands with a melancholy sigh.

Margaret gazed up at the house-keeper's troubled face with dismay. "Oh, Mrs. Dow . . . how very sad . . ."

Sara and Jenny had knocked their snowman down and caught up handfuls of snow to throw at each other. Jenny was shrieking excitedly as she ran from Sara. At the far end of the yard now, her voice came to the living room only faintly.

Margaret continued to sit, holding the envelope helplessly. She did not want to open it, to read whatever it was Jenny had written.

"Well, it's too bad." Mrs. Dow shook her head.

"I'll show it to Mr. Loring when he comes home," Margaret said at last. "And— thank you, Mrs. Dow."

When Mrs. Dow left the living room, Margaret sat a few minutes longer wondering what she should do. She wanted to call her husband at once. But, on second thought, he had work to do at the office, and a call would only upset him. There was nothing he could do if she did call. She decided to wait until he came home, and after a few more moments she got up and put the envelope on the mantel.

It was going to be hard waiting for Charles to come home. He would be so distressed, she was sure. And what could they do? . . . It was going to be a long day, keeping her secret.

Margaret picked up Jenny's blouse again and drew the thread through the button. She wanted to forget about the letter to Mrs. Loring, Clarion Hotel, Switzerland, but she knew that was impossible. She felt Evelyn Loring's presence everywhere, defeating her, closing the door on the future Margaret and Charles had planned so bravely.

In the afternoon Sara decided the tree needed more icicles, and she began adding strands one by one with a patience that caused Margaret to smile to herself as she watched.

Sara was such a serious girl. Everything she did was carefully done, neat, no nonsense. Margaret was sure Sara had been born tidy and tall and organized.

One by one Sara placed the icicles, standing back to admire her work. The tree glittered.

But Margaret was disappointed that Jenny didn't want to help. The little girl sat listlessly on the living-room floor, drooping her cheek on a hassock near the tree as she watched Sara work.

The afternoon was drawing to a close. Margaret longed for Mr. Loring's return, his cheerful voice and reassuring smile. Did other families have this low-ebb hour as twilight darkened the windows? It was more than just the letter to Switzerland. She needed him. "How are my girls?" he always said as he came into the entryway, bringing with him an aura of New York City and business meetings that had gone well.

She watched the clock. It hardly moved.

"Don't you want to help Sara put on the icicles?" Margaret stood by the hassock. She thought Jenny looked pale and tired.

48

She wished Charles would come and the day of waiting would be over.

"Jenny just throws them on," Sara objected, glancing over her shoulder. She was quite happy to be finishing the tree by herself. It was going to be absolutely wonderful when she was done. She didn't want Jenny throwing icicles on every which way.

"Jenny." Margaret bent down and tilted Jenny's face. "Why don't you go upstairs and have a rest before dinner?"

"I'm not tired."

Margaret hesitated. It was difficult to know how much to say, how much to insist. But Jenny did look wan. There was a dejected quality about the usually bright elfin face.

Perhaps it was only the excitement of the holidays, Margaret reasoned. Everyone got overexcited, and then overtired. Especially children. Especially high-strung children like Jenny.

Sara went on methodically draping icicles on the tree. There were already too many, Margaret thought, but she would never have said so. Sara worked on intently. And by and by Jenny straggled up from the floor and wandered away.

"I hope she's not coming down with something," Margaret murmured.

Sara had finished at last.

There was not an icicle left in the box. Now the tree was perfect.

Sara felt she deserved some refreshments after her work on the tree, and she found Jenny sitting at the kitchen table eating Christmas cookies. Crumbs stuck to Jenny's mouth and spilled on the table. The cookies were shaped like stars and bells and Christmas trees.

"Are you coming down with something?" Sara studied Jenny suspiciously. Maybe Jenny had caught the cold Sara had last week. Sara hoped no one would think of this; if Jenny got sick, it would seem like Sara's fault.

Sara wasn't ever very sick. Her colds were mild and far apart. But Jenny's health was more fragile, and she got put to bed almost at once if she said her throat was sore or her stomach hurt.

"She has a delicate constitution," Momma had always told people. "You know we almost lost her once."

Momma's words were spoken in a

hushed, mournful voice—always with a closing of eyes and a sigh of gratitude that the worst had not happened, that Momma and Daddy had not lost Jenny. But they almost had.

Sara had only been about six years old, but she remembered when Jenny was so sick. Momma and Daddy were at the hospital almost all the time. Sara had to play by herself. The house was empty, echoey with the silence of absent voices, absent footsteps. Sara trailed around after Mrs. Dow, lonely and forlorn.

When Jenny came home from the hospital at last, Momma sat by her crib. Tears glistened in her eyes. Tears of happiness that Jenny was better, that she wasn't going to die.

"My little Jenny-wren," Momma whispered, leaning close to the crib. That was when she began to call her Jenny-wren, the baby with soft downy hair and dimpled fingers.

Sara stood at the crib beside Momma, and Momma said, "She's like a little birdie. A little Jenny-wren. We must take good care of her. . . . Go and play quietly, Sara.

We must let our little Jenny-wren sleep."

Ever since then Momma and Daddy had worried about Jenny; Sara didn't want to get blamed if Jenny got sick. She sat down at the kitchen table beside Jenny. "We're going Christmas shopping tomorrow," she reminded her, a sort of don't-get-sick-*now* warning.

"I can eat more cookies than you." A flash of Jenny's impish smile restored Sara's confidence.

"No more cookies so close to suppertime." Mrs. Dow removed the plate briskly—but not before Sara had seized a cookie as the plate flew by. It was a delicious star sprinkled with red sugar. Tasting it was like going back through all the Christmases Sara could remember.

Jenny's face had grown thoughtful. "Can we get a present for Mr. Hoffman?"

"Mr. Hoffman's not here." Sara finished the red-sugar star and brushed her fingers neatly.

"He is too here. I saw him."

"No, you didn't."

"I did so. I did so, didn't I, Mrs. Dow?"

Mrs. Dow said she didn't know about that one way or the other.

It was time to pare the potatoes for dinner. Her work was never done.

7

When Mr. Loring arrived home, it was nearly six o'clock.

The woods glimmered with whiteness in the dusk. Lights shone from the windows of the house as he pulled his car into the driveway. The wind had fallen, and the evening was calm and clear.

Margaret was in the living room. The day had seemed never ending to her, and she was grateful that Sara and Jenny were upstairs so that she could show the letter to her husband without having to wait longer.

Mr. Loring came into the living room, rubbing his hands cheerfully, anticipating a pleasant evening at home, and Margaret hated to disrupt his happy mood.

"You haven't read it yet?" He looked at her with surprise when she gave him the letter and told him how Mrs. Dow had found it on the hall table.

"I thought you should be the one to read it."

Jenny was his child, not hers. Margaret had hoped, in time, to feel that Jenny was her child. But maybe that time would never come. Not while Jenny was still longing for her mother.

Mr. Loring tore open the envelope roughly. It was quite unlike him to do this. He always opened mail with the silver letter opener on the mantel. From the ragged edges he drew out the letter, written on a piece of the lined notebook paper school-children use.

> *Dear Momma*
> *Mr. Hoffman is back. I saw him.*
> *He didn't see me. Will you come*
> *home for Christmas? We have a*
> *big tree. Please come.*
>
> > *Jenny*

He handed the single sheet to Margaret, and she read the letter so trustingly addressed, placed on the hall table with the outgoing mail, needing a stamp. A letter to a woman who was dead, who was not coming back for Christmas or any other time.

"It's all starting again," Mr. Loring

said bleakly. He took the letter back from Margaret and read it again with a disheartened expression.

"Where did she get that address?" Margaret asked in a hushed voice.

"Evelyn wrote once from Zermatt, just after she arrived there. Jenny must have kept the postcard. Evelyn was at the Clarion Hotel."

Mr. Loring paused. His voice softened.

"She said it was very beautiful. Quaint. She could see the Matterhorn from her window. Jenny read the card to everyone she could find. Sara told her she was going to have it all worn out."

Margaret smiled faintly. Don't hurt me with your memories, she begged silently.

But Mr. Loring stood holding the letter, remembering. . . . It has a real stamp from Switzerland, Sara had said . . . They all watched the mail for more postcards. But there had only been that one.

Margaret waited, feeling more and more cut off, separated now from Charles, as well as from Jenny. She felt insignificant in their lives, unable to cope with memories of Evelyn Loring. Evelyn herself was in the room, ghostly, unseen, powerful.

By the windows the Christmas tree sparkled with reflections and color. Mr. Hoffman's wooden bird turned on the velvet ribbon, slowly, ever so slightly, blown by some small current of air. Icicles trembled, shining with light.

Hark, the herald angels sing . . . glory to the newborn king. . . .

"Sara seems to have adjusted so well." Margaret's voice trembled. She turned away so that Mr. Loring could not see her face.

Mr. Loring was aware of the quaver in Margaret's voice. He had hurt her, he thought, talking about Evelyn.

"Sara's older; I expect that helps," he said lamely.

He hadn't wanted to hurt Margaret, not for anything in the world. He touched her shoulder gently. "Please don't be upset. Everything will work out."

"Yes, of course it will." Margaret tried to steady her voice. Mrs. Dow was bringing in the afternoon coffee.

"Maybe sending Jenny away to school

is the answer." Mr. Loring spoke without particular conviction. He did not know what the answer was. He realized that Mrs. Dow had probably heard what he said, but he knew from years of experience that family matters were safe with her. He watched her departing figure, her straight back and firm step, with fondness.

Margaret turned from the windows where she had been gazing at a landscape on the brink of night, sparkling with snow, a border of trees melting into the blackness of the sky.

Mr. Loring stood by the fireplace, still holding the letter.

> *Mrs. Loring*
> *Clarion Hotel*
> *Switzerland*

"I don't see much point in confronting Jenny with this, do you? She'd just deny it, like she denied writing in the book. Talking to her doesn't seem to accomplish anything."

"No, it doesn't," Margaret agreed regretfully. "It just upsets everybody."

Mr. Loring wadded the letter and

threw it into the fire. Flames curled around it, charring the edges, until it caught and flamed up a moment, and quickly turned to ashes.

8

Each year since Jenny had been about seven years old, she and Sara had gone into town a few days before Christmas to do their shopping.

It was the best time to go. The stores were glowing with lights and tinsel. There was a special holiday bustle along the streets. It was almost Christmas!

Sara had written a list in her prim, neat handwriting:

> "slippers for Daddy
> stationery for Margaret
> candy for Mrs. Dow
> a flower vase for Aunt Irene
> cigars for Uncle Martin"

She had saved her allowance for several months. She was ready.

"I'm not sure you should go out, Jenny," Margaret said at breakfast. She thought Jenny still looked pale and tired.

"Please." Jenny snuggled close to Margaret's chair and looked at Margaret with beseeching eyes. Margaret put her hand on Jenny's arm. It felt very small under the sleeve of a sweater slightly too large, turned up at the cuffs.

"You wouldn't want to get sick at Christmastime," Margaret said, but it was hard to say no to Jenny. With her head slightly to one side, Jenny gazed at Margaret adoringly, as if she already knew Margaret would grant her any wish.

"I'm going to buy something beautiful for you." Jenny's voice was almost a whisper.

"Is that so?" Margaret gazed back, deep into Jenny's eyes.

"Yes, I am," Jenny promised, leaning close.

Margaret hesitated.

"The most beautiful present in the whole store."

Margaret laughed. There was no resisting Jenny.

"Well, let me see now. You really can't walk, it's too far in this cold."

Mists of frost glazed the windowpanes.

All the world beyond the room was cold with snow and ice.

"I'll tell you what we'll do."

Jenny lifted her face sweetly.

"I have some books to return to the library. I'll drive you in this afternoon and wait at the library for you."

"Oh, goody—" Jenny broke and ran away, just when Margaret wanted to give her a hug and a kiss. She was like a will-o'-the-wisp, hard to catch and hold, always fluttering off to a world of her own.

"I suppose it will be all right." Margaret turned to Sara for some confirmation that her decision was sound. Charles had left early that morning, so there was no one to consult but Sara.

"Oh, sure." Sara spread jam on toast, careful to cover the edges. She had only worried for a moment—when Margaret first said Jenny couldn't go. When Jenny began to beg, Sara knew everything would be all right. Long ago Sara had learned that when something was denied, Jenny could get it for them.

"It's too cold to sled today," Momma said.

"Much too cold," Daddy agreed.

"*You ask.*" Sara put her mouth close to Jenny's ear.

"*Please, Momma, please, Daddy—just for a little while?*" There was such a tremor of longing in Jenny's voice.

"*All right, then, just for a little while.*"

It had always worked.

When Margaret left them at the stores, Sara pulled her Christmas list out of her pocket. This was rather unnecessary, as she knew every item by heart. Nevertheless she consulted the list gravely, as though seeing it for the first time.

"Let's go to the candy store and get Mrs. Dow's candy."

Jenny held tight to Sara's hand, and they made their way along the busy street among the other shoppers.

"Maybe we'll see Mr. Hoffman," Jenny confided. She had forgotten her own Christmas list, so she had nothing to consult.

Sara didn't answer. She couldn't see the use of answering.

Jenny tugged at Sara's hand. "Maybe that's him—"

Sara looked with surprise. Jenny was

pointing to a street-corner Santa Claus, ringing a large shiny bell.

"That's not Mr. Hoffman," Sara said, pulling Jenny along.

"Maybe under the beard." Jenny looked back over her shoulder hopefully.

"That man is way too tall to be Mr. Hoffman," Sara declared.

Jenny hurried along, her hand in Sara's. But she kept looking for men who weren't so tall.

After they had bought all of their gifts except the ones for each other, they came to the time of their shopping trip when they always separated for a few minutes.

"I'll meet you right back here," Sara said at the entrance of the big Woolworth store.

Inside the entrance a blast of heat warmed incoming shoppers.

People were having coffee and sandwiches at a counter.

A large table in the aisle was heaped with mistletoe in plastic-wrapped packages.

Jenny vanished into the crowd, and Sara walked toward the toy counters. She was going to buy Jenny a box of Make-

Your-Own-Beads she had seen there a few weeks before.

When they met again, their shopping was finished.

"I didn't see Mr. Hoffman," Jenny said in a discouraged voice. She had looked for Mr. Hoffman among the crowds, but she hadn't seen him anywhere.

"Should we buy him a present?"

"We have to meet Margaret at the library." Sara looked at Jenny. She wished Jenny had found Mr. Hoffman—but of course Jenny couldn't. Mr. Hoffman wasn't here. It was all a mistake.

"Sara?" Jenny was waiting for an answer.

"We don't have any money left."

Jenny pulled a mitten off with her teeth and showed Sara three dimes and a quarter in her hand.

"We can't buy anything with that," Sara said.

"We can buy *some*thing."

"No, we can't."

Sara had about all the packages she could carry. Her arms were heavy. And she was getting hungry.

"We've got to go home and have supper."

Jenny sighed and pulled her mitten on, but they were no sooner out of the store when she cried, "There he is—there's Mr. Hoffman!"

She darted away, clutching her paper bag with Sara's gift—and Sara had no choice but to run after her so they wouldn't get separated.

But wouldn't it be wonderful to see Mr. Hoffman!

It was hard to run along the crowded sidewalks, but Sara kept sight of Jenny. And she saw the short, stocky figure of an old man not far ahead.

"Jenny—wait—" Sara called.

But Jenny darted around a woman and on through the crowd.

Sara was not far behind when Jenny caught up with Mr. Hoffman.

"Mr. Hoffman—Mr. Hoffman—" Jenny grabbed his arm, and Mr. Hoffman turned.

But it wasn't Mr. Hoffman.

A strange face stared down at Jenny, and she stood looking up with astonishment, her hand still clutching the man's coat sleeve.

The man was not at all like Mr. Hoffman. He had a white moustache and round eyeglasses with thin gold rims. There was no kindly smile as he looked down at the mitten clutching his arm.

Jenny, suddenly frightened to have caught hold of a stranger, released the sleeve and backed away, stepping on Sara's foot.

"I thought it was him," Jenny tried to explain as the man disappeared in the crowd.

Sara was disappointed too. "Well, it wasn't." She shifted her packages, trying to get a free hand to take Jenny's hand. "Now come *on*. We're already late."

"I thought it was Mr. Hoffman." Jenny had to run to keep up, Sara was pulling her along so fast.

Once they were off the main street where the stores were, the sidewalks were deserted. The houses along the street were surrounded by snowy lawns. Christmas-tree lights had already been turned on in a few front windows. But Sara and Jenny didn't notice the lights.

"Don't you wish it was Mr. Hoffman?" Jenny tried to keep up with Sara.

"Yes, I wish it was." Sara looked straight ahead.

After that they didn't talk anymore. The cold was increasing, and the three blocks to the library seemed a long, desolate stretch. They had found Mr. Hoffman and lost him, all in a moment.

9

At the house Mrs. Dow was preparing dinner. A casserole bubbled behind the glass door of the oven; wooden bowls had been set out for salad. But she took time from her work to see the presents Sara and Jenny had bought as Sara unloaded the bags on the kitchen table.

"See—these are slippers for Daddy—and stationery for Margaret. . . ." Sara named off the gifts with solemn importance, regarding each one with satisfaction.

"Isn't that nice?" Mrs. Dow stood at the table, nodding as each item appeared.

"And here's a vase for Aunt Irene to put flowers in." Sara carefully took a green glass vase from a box padded with white tissue paper. "Isn't that beautiful? Oh—and here's a box of incense for Daddy. A lady in the store was burning it. It smells just like Christmas trees."

Tiny scented brown cones stood like

soldiers in a row in a gaudy red-and-gold box.

"Very fancy," Mrs. Dow declared.

"I thought I saw Mr. Hoffman, but it wasn't him." Jenny spread her arms on the table and slumped down on them dejectedly.

"Maybe you'll see him another time," Mrs. Dow suggested.

"Do you think so?" Jenny looked up at Mrs. Dow hopefully. "We ran after a man, but it wasn't Mr. Hoffman."

"It was just an old man," Sara said. She wasn't going to show how disappointed she was. Hadn't she known all along Mr. Hoffman wasn't really here? She rustled a bag, pushing Jenny's bead kit down into the bottom. She couldn't show that to Mrs. Dow now.

"If he's back, you'll be seeing him," Mrs. Dow said matter-of-factly. She nudged Jenny's arm. "Show me what you bought."

Most of the things were already on the table, but Jenny poked around in the nearly empty bags and found Uncle Martin's handkerchief and a box of perfumed soap for Margaret. At the bottom of another bag was Mrs. Dow's candy. Jenny squashed shut the top of the bag and began to laugh. "You can't see this one! You can't see this one!"

She hugged the crinkly brown paper bag and hopped around the kitchen.

"You can't see this one! You can't see this one!"

"That's the very one I want to see." Mrs. Dow put on a stern, ferocious face.

"No, no, no!" Jenny shrieked. "It's a dreadful monster. If I let it out of the bag, it will eat you up."

"Mercy!" Mrs. Dow clapped her hands to her face and looked quite frightened.

"It has six eyes and six hundred legs."

Mrs. Dow retreated several steps.

"It's a terrible monster."

"Get it out of my kitchen." Mrs. Dow shook her apron at Jenny and the brown paper bag—and Jenny ran away to hide Mrs. Dow's candy under her bed.

Mrs. Dow lowered her apron and stood silent a moment with a musing expression. Sara, having displayed her purchases, began to put them carefully back into the bags; but she was watching Mrs. Dow. Mrs. Dow knew things. Lots of things. Sara wondered how much Mrs. Dow *did* know, but she didn't ask right away. She put her bags on a chair by the table and sat down to pull off her boots.

There was a small rug by the kitchen door where wet boots were supposed to dry.

Jenny had run off through the house trailing snow, but Sara put her boots on the rug.

Then she stood unbuttoning her coat slowly, watching Mrs. Dow. Mrs. Dow peered into the oven at the casserole, and the oven door closed with a soft swishing sound.

"Do you think Jenny will have to go away to school?"

Mrs. Dow looked around with surprise.

"Why do you think I can answer that?"

Sara hesitated. "I just thought you'd know."

Mrs. Dow turned her back and began to wash celery at the sink. She didn't seem inclined to talk, and Sara stood absently pushing at a spoon that lay on the table.

After what seemed a long time, Mrs. Dow said, "Maybe she will, and maybe she won't. Time will tell."

"Mr. Hoffman's still in Germany, I bet," Sara said.

Mrs. Dow didn't answer.

"Jenny keeps looking for him."

Mrs. Dow set celery to drain on a towel. The clock above the stove ticked into the silence.

"And she keeps waiting for Momma to come back. Maybe she'll have to go away."

Mrs. Dow turned at last. Sara's eyes were luminous, troubled, and Mrs. Dow felt a sadness for her, for all the family. Even the rich people had problems.

"Don't start worrying about things before they happen."

"But suppose it happens?"

Mrs. Dow didn't know quite how to answer that.

"Suppose it happens?" Sara persisted.

"It's only two days to Christmas." Mrs. Dow turned back to the salad. "It's not the time to be talking about gloomy things."

When Sara had gone, bearing away her parcels, the housekeeper was still at the sink chopping celery and carrots. But she couldn't get Sara's questions out of her mind. What would the house be like without

Jenny prattling about monsters with six hundred legs? Without Jenny rushing through the kitchen waving her elbows? *"I'm a fish, Mrs. Dow—I'm a fish."*

Or Jenny huddling on her knees over a pan of water, lapping it with her tongue. *"I'm a doggie and this is my supper."*

She was a troll living under a kitchen-table-bridge.

An airplane circling the lawn for a landing.

In the summer she was a bumblebee. Or a flower. She would stand with clenched fists, slowly unfolding the petals of her fingers.

In the winter she was the Snow Queen, rolling in the snow until she was white from head to foot, calling Mrs. Dow to come to the back door and see.

Mrs. Dow could not imagine the house without Jenny.

The thought was still on her mind when Mr. Dow came to pick her up at seven thirty. She saw the old blue car pull into the driveway, gleaming with light, puffing exhaust into the cold night air.

It was time to go home.

*　　*　　*

Mrs. Dow liked to get off her feet in the evenings. When Mr. Dow's supper was over, she would put on a pair of warm, limp bedroom slippers. She made herself a cup of tea so strong and black Mr. Dow said it looked like coffee.

"How's your coffee?" he would ask, settling into his armchair and opening the newspaper. There were always interesting things to be discovered in the newspaper.

Mr. Dow had a small auto-repair shop. People in town said if Mr. Dow couldn't fix your car, no one could. And his rates were very reasonable. He could have charged more, but he didn't.

The Dow house was in town, on Cedar Street.

It was small, cozy, brimming with furniture and bric-a-brac. In the dining room, ornamental plates lined a narrow ledge. The kitchen clock was in the shape of a yellow daisy flourishing its petals cheerfully.

In the living room, arms of chairs were lacy with Mrs. Dow's crocheting. The rug was worn into familiar paths. There was a white china owl with a clock on its chest—a souvenir Mr. Dow had brought back from somewhere long ago.

It was all dear and beloved.

On this evening, Mrs. Dow sipped her hot black tea and allowed herself a sigh. Then another sigh.

Lamplight reflected in the windows that looked out on Cedar Street. The rooms still smelled of supper, warm and fragrant.

Mr. Dow listened to two or three sighs, and then lowered his newspaper.

"What's bothering you, dear?" He peered over his eyeglasses and saw Mrs. Dow's face was set into lines of concern.

"I've done something, and I'm not sure if it was right," Mrs. Dow said. "Maybe I've meddled in something that was none of my business."

Mr. Dow raised his eyebrows and waited with some amusement. He had been married to Mrs. Dow for nearly forty years, and she never meddled in other people's affairs. He could not think of one instance in forty years.

Mrs. Dow sighed again and set off, as far as Mr. Dow could tell, on another subject entirely.

"They're thinking of sending the little one away."

"They" always meant the Loring

family. Mr. Dow understood that. But "away"—what did that mean?

"Away? Away where?" Mr. Dow frowned.

"Away to school. Because of her mother, you know."

"Ah." Mr. Dow nodded thoughtfully. He knew how the little Loring girl didn't believe her mother was dead. At least not at first.

"I thought she'd gotten over that," he said.

"So did I." Mrs. Dow gazed across the room sadly. "But it's all started up again, the talk about sending her away."

"Why is that, after all this time?" Mr. Dow's face, full of lines from all the years of living, was sympathetic.

"For one thing, she wrote a letter. I found it on the hall table when I was dusting. I knew her handwriting at once, but the address gave me a start. It was to her mother, to Switzerland."

Mr. Dow thought this was sad news. He rubbed his chin, and shook his head to think of a little girl writing a letter to a mother dead almost a year.

Mr. and Mrs. Dow had never had any

children of their own, and through the years Mrs. Dow had worked for the Loring family they had both developed an affection for the Loring girls. Mr. Dow often carried candies for them in his pockets when he drove out to get Mrs. Dow at the end of the day. One evening he had brought a dozen balloons and tied them into two bunches, one for Sara and one for Jenny. It was summertime, when the early evenings were bright with the lingering radiance of the setting sun.

Sara and Jenny ran back and forth across the grass, holding the balloons high above their heads.

Then Jenny, the little one, had let her balloons go one by one, to see how high they would float.

Only one balloon had burst against a tree branch. The others rose up over the trees and the road, and went away into the evening sky. Jenny stood with rapture watching the balloons sail away. It had been a wonderful sight to see. . . .

"And she thinks Mr. Hoffman has come back," Mrs. Dow continued.

"What—old Hoffman back from Germany?" Mr. Dow had not heard of this.

"He isn't really," Mrs. Dow said quickly. "They went to his house, but no one was there. It was all a mistake. But she's thinking of her mother again, don't you see? And about the way things used to be."

Mr. Dow rubbed his chin again. The newspaper lay neglected on his knees.

After a moment Mrs. Dow said confidingly, "I got to thinking today about all the years I've been with the Lorings, watching those girls grow up. It was a sad thing that Mrs. Loring died, and she'd be sorry to think that her baby was to be sent away. She always favored the little one—not that that was right, mind you."

Mrs. Dow shook her head slowly.

Her lean fingers picked at a doily on the chair arm.

"That wasn't right, but it was the only fault she had. Mr. Loring was the same way. It wasn't right, but I guess they couldn't help it."

And if the truth were told, Mrs. Dow knew in her heart that she favored Jenny too. It was somehow so much easier to love small, elfin little girls like Jenny than tall, prim, quiet girls like Sara. Sara never ran up behind Mrs. Dow and untied her apron strings and said the fairies did it. Sara never threw her arms around Mrs. Dow's waist and laughed up at her, chanting "I love you—I love you—I love you—can we make cookies?"

Her thoughts were interrupted by Mr. Dow's gentle prodding: "What is it you've done that you're worried about?"

Mrs. Dow sighed reluctantly and left the room a moment, her soft slippers making no sound on the carpet. She went down the short hallway to the bedroom and was back almost at once carrying her handbag, a sturdy practical black pocketbook of imitation leather, containing many compartments. She sat down again with the handbag in her lap and opened the clasp with a resounding snap. She pushed at things here and there inside the bag while Mr. Dow waited curiously; at last she took out a small spray of green leaves.

"Mistletoe," she said, holding the spray in her fingers and studying it anxiously.

Mr. Dow leaned forward. Lamplight fell on his ruddy face and thick white hair. The newspaper slipped aside, crinkling slightly as he moved.

"It was just after dinner tonight. I was clearing up in the dining room and I saw mistletoe hanging in the archway that goes to the hall, just like Mrs. Loring always hung it at Christmastime."

Mrs. Dow looked across the lamplight at Mr. Dow to be sure he understood. "The first Mrs. Loring, not the new one."

Mr. Dow nodded to show he understood.

"Every Christmas Mrs. Loring put mistletoe up in the archway. And when I saw it there tonight, it surprised me. When I went closer, I could see that it had just been stuck up with a bit of tape. Not neat like Mrs. Loring did it. She always had lots more, big bunches of mistletoe. And she'd fasten up pine branches to fill in the archway. It was always very pretty."

Mrs. Dow paused a moment, dangling the skimpy bit of mistletoe to which a small strip of sticky tape still clung.

"I could hear them all laughing about something in the living room, Mr. and Mrs. Loring and the girls, and I wondered what would happen when Mr. Loring saw the mistletoe. There'd be trouble, I thought. I could see the hall chair wasn't quite in the right place, like it had been dragged to the archway to stand on and then not put back right."

"So you took down the mistletoe?"

Mrs. Dow looked at her husband guiltily. "Maybe I was wrong to do it. You can't sweep things under the rug forever."

She was silent a moment.

"I just thought—well, there they were, all so happy, and it's been a sad year for Mr. Loring and the girls. Let them have a happy evening, I said to myself. Let them have a happy Christmas."

"I think you did just right," Mr. Dow said comfortingly.

Mrs. Dow touched the mistletoe tentatively. "I don't know. It got me to thinking of her again so strong, to see it dangling there. It was like a ghost had done it."

It sounded foolish, but that was how she had felt when she saw the mistletoe. That a ghost had come unseen and unheard through the rooms—to put the mistletoe in the archway.

"She used to string colored lights across the archway too, in the pine branches and mistletoe."

Mrs. Dow's voice drifted back over the years.

"Oh, it was pretty. And here was just this little bit of mistletoe put up hastily. I knew no ghost had done it. So I took it down and put it in my pocketbook and never said a word to anybody."

10

✦✦ By midmorning Christmas Eve day, a heavy snow began to fall.

Jenny thought it was exciting. She could hardly see the trees on the lawn or the gateposts at the end of the driveway. She stood by the living-room windows and stared out at the white fairyland. It was like being in the paperweight globe Momma had with a tiny house and tiny trees inside.

"Shake the globe, Jenny-wren."

Soft, swirling snow filled the glass ball.

"Momma, how does the snow get in there?"

"That's a secret only the fairies know."

"I'm a fairy, Momma."

"No you're not. You're my Jenny-wren."

"I'm a fairy, a snow fairy."

Sara came, and stood by the door.

"Can Sara be a snow fairy too?"

Momma laughed. All her clothes were soft and bright. Light glistened on the golden earrings she wore. She was going to a party with Daddy. The cars were coming soon.

The world was full of snow and snow fairies. . . .

And now, today it was the same.

Jenny leaned close to the window. Remembering.

Margaret found the snow less enchanting. She knew it would make driving difficult, and she worried that the guests invited for Christmas Eve dinner might not be able to come. Aunt Irene and Uncle Martin lived in town. That wasn't too far, but far enough if the roads were impassable. The Forester family lived even farther away.

Margaret sat by the bedroom window in her dressing gown, drawing a brush through her soft yellow hair. Laid out on the flower-patterned bedspread were the skirt and blouse she would put on for the day. There would be a pretty dress for evening.

Snowflakes fell by the thousands. No

two alike, which was wonderful, of course; but would they never stop?

And there was something more. Something Margaret could not define as easily as she could define her concern about the weather. It was a vague, nagging sense that something would go wrong, something over which she had no control. And this sense of uneasiness persisted when she went downstairs at last and saw Jenny at the living-room windows gazing out at the snow.

The little girl stood silent, dreaming, her back turned, her long loose hair falling about her shoulders.

What would Margaret see if she took those thin little shoulders and turned Jenny around to face her?

Jenny stood so still. Jenny, who was usually skipping and darting about, chattering in her whimsical way.

Margaret paused in the doorway uncertainly. There was a silence in the room deepened by the heavy veil of snow which fell past the windows, and she hesitated to disturb the motionless child who was somehow like a person in a photograph caught forever in a moment of time.

Without speaking to Jenny, she left

the doorway and wandered restlessly here and there about the house, hoping at each window to see that the snow had stopped.

"Oh, Charles," she mourned, sinking into a chair in the study, "what if they can't come?"

The view from the study window was obscured by the falling snow. At the edge of the woods trees loomed ghostlike through the shroud of white. The world was vanishing.

Stop, please stop, Margaret prayed.

"Mrs. Dow has gone to so much work ... everything's planned." She looked at her husband for sympathy.

"They'll get here," he assured her cheerfully. "Irene and Martin haven't missed a Christmas Eve in ten years."

Margaret smiled halfheartedly. She was still praying *not now, now that I'm the new Mrs. Loring—let's not start our Christmas festivities with a terrible snowstorm and no guests.*

After lunch Jenny and Sara hovered around in the kitchen watching Mrs. Dow's preparations for the company dinner that night. The snow was still coming down outside, and Jenny wanted to run out into the full, deep whiteness of the snow. Every bush and tree branch was heavy with snow. Every windowsill was stacked high. A wind had risen, driving the snow against the house in fierce waves.

"Is this a blizzard?" Jenny asked.

Mrs. Dow said maybe so.

"Let's go out, Sara." Jenny caught her sister's hand.

"You can't go out in this," Mrs. Dow was quick to say.

Sara pulled her hand from Jenny's. "We'd get lost out there. We can't even see the end of the driveway."

Jenny wanted to go out, but nobody would let her. Not Sara or Mrs. Dow. Not Margaret. Not even Daddy.

She ran to the study to ask. "Please, Daddy." She lifted her head beguilingly.

But Daddy said, "Not today, Jenny." He had papers on his desk. He was busy even now, even on Christmas Eve day.

Jenny went away with lagging steps. If Momma were here, she would let Jenny go out and play in the great blizzard. Jenny was sure of that. But Momma wasn't here.

About three o'clock the snow grew thin

and stopped. Wind sighed in the tree branches. Shortly after, the snowplow from town came along the road, slowly pushing the snow into banks on either side. And Sara and Jenny went out at last, making deep tracks as they waded through the thick snow that lay across the lawn.

They were still outside when Mr. Dow came for Mrs. Dow at four o'clock. She was going home early because it was Christmas Eve, and she was to have a holiday too.

It was nearing twilight, but the countryside, glowing with whiteness, marked by the thin blue shadows of trees, seemed illumined in the last rays of light before darkness fell. The wind had died down. The storm was over, and a hush had settled upon the white winter woods.

Margaret had packed a shopping bag with food and presents for Mrs. Dow to take home, and the housekeeper came out of the kitchen door bundled up in a heavy coat and boots, with a warm scarf tied around her head.

She proceeded cautiously through the snow as Mr. Dow came to meet her, took the shopping bag and stowed it in the backseat of the old blue car. Jenny and Sara came running to say good-by and Merry Christmas to Mrs. Dow. They knew their box of candy was somewhere in the knobby, bulging bag Mr. Dow had already whisked out of sight. They knew Mrs. Dow's presents for them—*to Jenny from Santa Claus* . . . *to Sara from Santa Claus*—had been sneaked under the Christmas tree in the living room for them to discover Christmas morning. It had always been that way.

Mrs. Dow stood by the car, adjusting her scarf.

"Everything's done," she said. "You girls help tonight."

She saw their faces close to her, pushing into her memory to stay forever: Sara thin and solemn, Jenny with a tilt to her mouth. Their cheeks were bright with cold. Caps were pulled down tight over their ears.

"I'm going to help serve," Sara said.

"Me too." Jenny hung on the door handle and rubbed at snow on the car window.

"That's good. You girls have a nice Christmas." Mrs. Dow gathered her coat and settled herself in the front seat of the

car. She would not be back until after
Christmas.

Sara and Jenny stood at the edge of
the driveway and waved after the car.
When it reached the road, Mr. Dow waved
back. They could just barely tell through
the snowy windows.

"Merry Christmas," Jenny shouted
one last time. She waved her arms franti-
cally and jumped up and down in the snow.
"Merry Christmas, Mrs. Dow."

But by then the car had already disappeared down the road.

11

The road was plowed, the guests arrived. But with this problem solved, new worries crept into Margaret's mind. Past Christmases filled the rooms, pressing close about her, Christmases before she had ever known Charles Loring. Evelyn's Christmases.

Voices from those years whispered in the air. Memories, like ghosts, lurked in the hallways and crowded around the long, candlelit table.

Was Charles remembering? Was he only pretending to be the cheerful host? Margaret looked toward him down the table shimmering with water goblets. Was he remembering?

Was his sister Irene comparing how things had been when Evelyn sat at the end of the table on Christmas Eve?

Were the Foresters remembering?

Were Jenny and Sara longing for a face they would never see again?

Everybody seemed happy . . . but Margaret wished she could be sure.

When it was time to serve the cake Mrs. Dow had baked, room was cleared by Margaret's place. Sara brought the cake from the kitchen, three layers frosted white and trimmed with red. Flames burned bright on the tall green candles beside the centerpiece of gilded pine cones. All the table was radiant with the glow of chandelier and candlelight.

Irene, plump and pink-cheeked, a small sequin Christmas wreath pinned to her dress, said she could not eat dessert. Heavens no! Wasn't she too fat already?

"I think you're just right," Jenny said lovingly. "You can have some cake."

"I don't know." Aunt Irene looked tempted.

"Mrs. Dow made it special," Jenny coaxed.

"Mrs. Dow is a wonderful cook, I know." Aunt Irene nodded around the table wisely. "Evelyn always said . . ." Her voice faded off apologetically. ". . . that Mrs. Dow was a wonderful cook."

Margaret looked down at the cake helplessly. The other Christmases *were* here.

Everybody remembered them. What would happen now?

But Jenny was giggling. "I want a big piece. This big—" She spread her arms as wide as she could, nearly upsetting a water glass. Uncle Martin said he didn't know if it was safe to sit near Jenny, and Margaret sliced the silver knife through the frosting of the Christmas cake. "Maybe just a small piece, Irene?"

Mrs. Forester, a fashionably slender lady, accepted her cake absently. "I don't like all this snow," she remarked. "Next year I'm going to Florida for the winter."

"You say that every year," her husband reminded her.

"Next year I just might do it."

"I'll go with you," Aunt Irene said promptly. "There's no snow in Florida."

"To Florida." Mr. Loring lifted his coffee cup.

It was all the usual light-hearted table talk. Margaret cut the cake and passed down the plates. Sara came from the kitchen with a fresh carafe of coffee. She carried it carefully, her dark eyes solemn and proud.

"At least coffee has no calories," Aunt Irene said cheerfully.

Sara went around the table, pausing at the side of each high-backed chair to pour coffee. Jenny watched Mrs. Forester push frosting aside on her plate; Mrs. Forester considered frosting too rich to eat.

Uncle Martin launched into a long story with a funny ending, and Mrs. Forester scooped up her frosting and put it on Jenny's plate.

Later, when the guests were leaving, Irene lingered behind the others, holding Margaret's hand in an affectionate and reassuring way. "I had a lovely time, Margaret."

It was Irene who had wanted Sara and Jenny to have "a woman in the house," a new mother, so to speak. As far as Irene could see, it was working out perfectly. Things did work out; Irene firmly believed that.

A cold draft of air came into the entry through the half-open door. A car engine was starting in the driveway. Sara and Jenny clung close to Aunt Irene, whose face, lighted by the entry lamp, was aglow with rosy shadows. The upturned collar of her coat brushed her earrings.

"How did you know a vase was just what I wanted for Christmas?"

"Santa Claus told us," Jenny chanted. "Santa Claus told us."

Irene smiled at Margaret over Jenny's head. Of course Santa Claus would speak to little girls like Jenny.

And then the company was gone, driving off into the frosty night.

The clock chimed a late hour into the empty hallway.

Margaret was the last to go upstairs to bed. She turned off the living-room lamps and the Christmas-tree lights and stood in the darkened room lighted only by the whiteness of snow beyond the windows.

The evening had really gone very well, and she wondered why she felt a sense of sadness sweeping over her. She should be happy. She had so much to be grateful for in her life.

And it was Christmas. The time of all times for happiness.

But the sadness was there, as though, alone in the dark room, she was looking down a corridor of years into some unknown anguish.

What secret is here that I don't know? she thought.

No answer came.

Outside, over the woods, a pale moon shone down on the nighttime land radiant with the wintry whiteness left by the snow.

On Christmas morning the snow began again. Mr. Loring noticed it first.

"Maybe Letty Forester won't wait for next year," he said. "Maybe she'll pack her bag and head right off for Florida now."

Margaret had been up early to fix a special Christmas breakfast. She was sitting gratefully in a chair by the tree watching Sara and Jenny open the last of their gifts. She was beginning to feel the strain of her pre-Christmas preparations, and she was glad to rest in the soft cushiony chair just doing nothing for a while.

"It's beads," Jenny said. She had torn the wrapping paper from Sara's gift, and there was the glossy blue cardboard box rattling hard inside with colored glass beads waiting to be strung.

"That's nice," Margaret said. "You can make me a necklace."

Sara was opening her last present. She had put it aside for last because she knew what it was by the shape of the box, and she didn't really want to open it at all. But at last everything else had been opened. She drew off the ribbon and lifted the cover of the box. Firelight flashed along the shiny blades of new skates, lighting memories of dark cold water and splitting ice. Every year she got new skates because she had never told anyone that she hated the pond, that she was afraid of the thin far places even when she stayed close to shore.

They had taken her out of the water and carried her to Mr. Hoffman's cottage. He had just been there by the pond, watching the skaters. No one even knew who he was.

But then he said he lived "just through the trees there," and Daddy had carried Sara, limp and shivering, dazed with fright.

"This is kind of you," Momma had said—hardly noticing the simple rooms she would eventually get to know so well. She took off Sara's wet clothes and wrapped her in a blanket, and brought her back out into Mr. Hoffman's little parlor to get warm by the fire.

And that was how they had met Mr. Hoffman. Sara, still panicky and bewildered, had at first thought of him as towering and tall, bristling with whiskers, bending over to peer at her from eyes half hidden by bushy brows. He was not really tall, but he had seemed to be because Sara was so little then. She stood huddled in the blanket, tears streaming down her cheeks.

Daddy sat on a chair holding Jenny in his lap. It was one of Jenny's first times to be out since she had been so sick. She was not quite three years old. She bumped her feet against Daddy's legs and put her hands out playfully toward the fire.

"You gave us a scare, Sara," Momma scolded. She shifted her fur coat back on her shoulders and looked at Sara.

"We called you back," Daddy said severely. "Why didn't you listen?"

After that he said Sara couldn't go skating for a week because she hadn't obeyed.

Sara never wanted to go skating again

ever. But Daddy had only punished her for a week.

And every year she got new skates. . . .

"I've got skates too." Jenny had opened another present. She sat cross-legged on the floor, surrounded by Christmas bows and wrapping paper, a few beads already strung for a necklace, fluffy bedroom slippers, a book about birds—all the wonderful things of Christmas morning.

"The ice should be good now, with all this cold weather we've had," Mr. Loring said. "You girls will have to get out there and show Margaret what good skaters you are."

"I'd like to see," Margaret agreed.

She had gotten up to kneel beside the tree, reaching to the back, where one last small package wrapped in white tissue paper had blended in too well with the circle of white felt laid around the base of the tree.

To my Jenny-wren from Momma

Margaret stared at the tag with dismay. *Something will go wrong,* she had thought. *Something will go wrong.* And now it had.

No one else was paying any attention. Jenny was trying to lace up a skate. Sara was neatly arranging her skates back into the box, her back turned.

Margaret remained a moment kneeling by the tree; the package with its childish writing *"To my Jenny-wren"* trembled in her hand. What shall I do? she wondered miserably. And then quickly, before the girls should notice, she took the package across the room to where Mr. Loring sat at one end of the sofa, watching Jenny struggle with the laces of the skates.

He took the package with a smile that faded as he read the tag. His eyes met Margaret's briefly, then he slipped off the loosely tied ribbon and unrolled the tissue paper. A bottle of cheap cologne lay in the paper that rustled softly in his hands.

"What is it, Daddy?" Sara turned suddenly, holding her box of skates.

"Shaving lotion." Mr. Loring drew the paper up to hide the bottle. "Some nice shaving lotion. Thank you, Margaret."

He didn't know why he lied—except perhaps to preserve what was left of the special happiness of Christmas morning, to save himself Jenny's denials and tears. Later he put the cologne and the tag into a desk drawer in his study, and nothing more was said of it.

The day seemed endlessly long to him afterward. And to Margaret. They had things to speak of together, decisions to make. But today, Christmas day, wasn't the time.

Late that afternoon, through a softly falling snow, Mr. Loring drove the family to Aunt Irene's for a Christmas supper, and when they came back home, Sara and Jenny were allowed to stay up past their bedtime again. They cracked walnuts by the fireplace and the Christmas day, so long looked forward to, came to an end when the clock struck eleven and they all went to bed at last.

The house was silent under a starless night sky.

There would not be another Christmas day for a long time.

12

On the day after Christmas Sara carried her presents up to her room and arranged them on the windowseat. Her mood was somber. There was such a let-down feeling to the day after Christmas. Now all that was left were the dreary days of winter. All the pretty Christmas things packed away, the school bus on cold dark mornings, wind blowing snow in swirls across the road and the woods. Nothing ever changed. And Sara wanted things to change.

It was snowing again. Had Mrs. Forester gone to Florida?

Were airport attendants juggling Mrs. Forester's luggage on their carts?

A loudspeaker would announce: *Flight 509 . . . boarding now. . . .*

Good-by, Mrs. Forester.

Sara put the box of skates in her closet. She didn't want to look at them on the windowseat. Too soon Daddy would say, "Why don't you girls get out your skates?"

Jenny didn't have skates the day Sara fell through the ice. She was too little. She'd stayed near the bank, pretending to skate in her small fur-lined boots.

"Isn't she darling," Momma said, drawing up the soft dark collar of her coat.

"You're doing fine, Jenny," Daddy called.

"Look at me." Sara's voice drifted over the pond. "Look at me, everybody!"

Momma and Daddy looked for a moment. But it wasn't the same.

"I'm going out to the tree," Sara shouted, stroking off across the ice, already reflecting the long murky shadows of late afternoon.

At the middle of the pond a gnarled apple tree stood on a jutting strip of land.

The tree was too far away. As far away as the end of the world.

Only Sara was brave enough to go there.

Through the darkening afternoon their voices reached her across the ice: "Come back, Sara—come back."

But she flew on, exhilarated. Momma and Daddy were watching now. Watching *her*. No one else had gone as far as Sara was going. And Mommy and Daddy were watching her.

Jenny, skidding along on her boots, began to follow.

"Jenny!"

Sara heard Momma's voice, a frantic command blown by the wind.

"Jenny—Jenny!"

Jenny tottered and fell, sitting down in a tiny heap on the cold ice. But Sara raced boldly along. She was the only one brave enough to go to the tree. *Watch me, Momma. Watch me, Daddy.*

Past the other children.

Past big boys and big girls who were not as brave as little Sara.

Watch me, Momma. Watch me, Daddy.

The sun was gone. The afternoon was over. Soon it would be time to go home. The woods were washed with forlorn light. Leafless tree branches formed prickly patterns against the gray sky.

Sara felt the cold wind against her face . . . and she heard the creaking, scary sound of ice too thin to bear her weight.

But she could make it. The tree was close ahead. *Watch me, Momma. Watch me, Daddy.*

And then there was the giving way beneath her feet. The hushed, ominous splitting apart of thin ice. Nothing was there. Nothing to hold her. With a swift, wrenching movement the ice parted, gaping to show deep, icy water in the dull light of the fading afternoon.

"You gave us a scare," Momma said.

"You can't go skating for a week." Daddy was cross. "You were a naughty girl not to come back when we called."

But they hadn't really made much fuss. Not like when Jenny had been recovering from her sickness and Momma told Sara to play quietly.

"Go and play quietly, Sara. We must let our little Jenny-wren sleep."

Rooms of silence surrounded Sara. Lamps were lighted by late afternoon; Mrs. Dow was in the kitchen. Hallways were vast, lonesome places where Sara did not want to go.

"We must be quiet." Momma touched a finger to her lips to show that Sara mustn't talk. "Our little Jenny-wren has been so sick."

"What's my name, Momma?" Sara

looked up into Momma's face with longing. Momma was so beautiful.

But there was no special name for Sara. No Jenny-wren name for her. No way that Sara, thin and plain, could look like Momma. Everybody said Jenny had Momma's eyes, Momma's smile.

"Who do I look like?" Sara asked. Momma had come downstairs; her dress was soft and light, yellow with blue flowers scattered across.

Momma got out the photograph album, and Sara sat close, surrounded by Momma's perfume, feeling Momma's arm on her shoulders.

"Here—Cousin Mary." Momma pointed at a picture. "See, Sara, you look just like Cousin Mary."

Sara looked at the snapshot. She couldn't tell for sure. A hat shaded Cousin Mary's face. But either way, it wasn't the same as looking like Momma.

But Momma died. And Daddy married Margaret with her blue-gray eyes and soft yellow hair.

After that, Sara thought things would change. But they didn't change. Everything was the same as before. Margaret and

Daddy loved Jenny best, just like Momma and Daddy had loved Jenny best. They talked about sending Jenny away to school. Aunt Irene thought that was the answer. But nothing had ever come of it.

Then Jenny thought she saw Mr. Hoffman when she was on the school bus. It was a mistake, of course, but Daddy and Margaret started talking about the school again. And that gave Sara her idea: If Jenny went away to school, Margaret and Daddy would love Sara; she would be all they had. . . .

Margaret would wait for the school bus in the afternoon. Sara was coming home. "What did you do in school today, Sara?" Margaret would ask. . . . Daddy would be at his desk in the study. He would turn and smile at her. He had been waiting just for her to come.

Sara didn't want Daddy and Margaret to forget the school. She didn't want it to be forgotten as it was before. She wanted them to remember that Jenny was thinking about Momma, that Jenny needed a change, needed to be away from a house that was too full of memories.

Sara opened the drawer where she had

put the left-over ribbon and tissue paper from the bottle of cologne.

To my Jenny-wren from Momma.

"I want perfume too," Jenny had said last Christmas. She was leaning against Momma's knees as Momma unwrapped a gift of perfume from Daddy.

NIGHT STAR

The letters on the label were flourishing, flowing, full, like beautiful promises from an exotic land where ladies wore veils and men rode on horseback across desert sands to save the ladies and to love them.

"I want perfume too," Jenny breathed against Momma's cheek.

Sara had remembered. How could she forget, standing aside stiff and tall and gawky, holding a box of new skates while Momma and Jenny sprayed themselves with the sweet scent of NIGHT STAR.

It had been easy to imitate Jenny's handwriting. It had been easy to make the round, struggling letters of someone just learning to write instead of print. The letter to Switzerland. The verse in the book.

Remember Me When I Am Dead

> *Roses are blue*
> *Violets are red*
> *Remember me*
> *When I am dead*

Oh, I do remember you, Momma, Sara thought sadly. I remember everything. But you're gone now, and I want Daddy and Margaret to love *me*.

13

The afternoon was waning.

Gloomy light of a cloudy winter's day settled over Sara's room as she sat at her desk, smoothing a sheet of paper in the circle of light from the desk lamp.

Her presents were spread on the windowseat, by windows looking out upon the gray sky and the woods.

All her life Sara had seen those woods from her windows. She knew them cool and green in the summertime, yellow and red in autumn.

In winter the woods were black and white, like a charcoal drawing. In winter, all the color and brightness was indoors; Christmas-tree lights and party dresses and the best china set out for company on the dark-green Christmas cloth.

Christmas was such a wonderful, exciting time.

But it always ended. Too soon. Too

abruptly. One day it was Christmas. The next day everything was over.

And after Christmas she must always write thank-you notes. Momma had been very particular about that. . . . Dear Aunt Irene and Uncle Martin, thank you for the paint set. . . . Dear Aunt Julia, thank you for the sweater. How is California? Do you miss snow?

Through the years Sara had written many thank-you notes.

Jenny drew pictures instead, for her thank-you notes. People with big heads and sticklike arms ate candy, wore new dresses, held up new toys. Momma and Daddy loved these pictures.

"Jenny is so clever," Momma said.

But Sara wrote neat, dutiful notes.

Dear Mrs. Dow, thank you for the mittens you knit me.

Dear Mr. and Mrs. Forester, thank you for the sled.

"How do you spell Forester, Momma?"

Forester was a long name, when Sara was little.

But it wasn't thank-you notes Sara was thinking of now. The sheet of paper on her desk was only plain school notebook paper. Carefully, in the just-learning way Jenny had, Sara wrote:

Happy New Year Jenny-wren

She was going to put this on the breakfast table New Year's Day like Momma used to do. At every plate Momma always put a Happy New Year note.

*Happy New Year, Darling—*for Daddy
Happy New Year, Sara
Happy New Year, Jenny-wren

Always these three little greetings.

This New Year's Day there would be only one, by Jenny's place.

When Sara finished writing, she hid the paper in her school notebook. No one ever looked there. The paper would be safe until New Year's Day.

She went downstairs just as the mantel clock was striking four. The house was quiet. Through the living-room doorway she could see the Christmas-tree lights, snow falling at the windows. Daddy and Jenny

113

and Margaret were by the fireplace. It was like a Christmas-card picture—but not quite. There was a strange silence in the room, and Sara paused at the doorway uncertainly.

Jenny stood by Daddy's chair. She wore a blue jumper and a string of make-your-own-beads. Tears streaked her face.

No one spoke. Silence filled the room. And then Daddy said, "It's a nice school, Jenny. You'll like it." He took both of Jenny's hands in his to draw her close.

Sara clung by the doorway. A thousand thoughts raced through her mind at once.

It's a nice school, Jenny. You'll like it.

"Sara—" Margaret had noticed the movement by the door, and she stood up. "Come in, honey." She motioned toward Sara.

Daddy turned toward the door.

Jenny was watching through tears.

But still Sara hesitated.

It's a nice school, Jenny. You'll like it.

Everything she planned had come true.

"Come in, Sara," Daddy said. He held out his arm. He wanted to hold both Jenny and Sara in a circle of love; but Sara stayed by the door.

"What's the matter?" she asked, staring at Daddy and Margaret and Jenny. But she knew. She knew.

"Come in, Sara," Daddy said again, and Sara came a step closer. Fresh tears welled up in Jenny's eyes and flooded down her cheeks.

Sara felt Margaret's arm on her shoulder.

"Sara, we've just been telling Jenny about this wonderful school."

Of course. Sara's heart pounded. *Of course. Jenny must go away.*

Margaret's arm drew closer around Sara. Sara waited, and Margaret bent her head and spoke softly so no one else could hear.

"You know Jenny's been unhappy. This house has too many memories for her. She'll be happier at school."

Sara looked up into Margaret's eyes. The gentle gray-blue eyes were sad. Light glinted on the small silver necklace Margaret wore. Sara had no moment to feel apprehension, no time to realize that everything was not exactly as she had planned. There was no warning.

"Ashley Woods School," Margaret was saying. "And you'll be with her, Sara, so she won't feel too alone."

Sara stood rigidly in the circle of Margaret's arm.

No—not me—just Jenny. Not me—not me.

No one heard the silent cry; but Margaret saw Sara's face grow pale, her dark eyes fill with amazement, and she touched Sara's cheek tenderly. "You'll like the school, Sara," she said softly.

"Of course you'll like it." Daddy had overheard. He swung in his chair, facing Sara. "I was just telling Jenny that the girls go horseback riding and on overnight campouts. Doesn't that sound like fun?"

Sara wasn't listening. She twisted away from Margaret and stared blankly at the Christmas tree.

Mr. Hoffman's little bird hung motionless, as though it had forgotten how to fly.

Light glistened in the ornaments, upon the long silvery strands of the icicles Sara had put on so carefully on an afternoon that already seemed long, long ago.

At the windows snow fell softly and steadily into the winter afternoon.

"You'll really like it, Sara," Margaret said. "Daddy and I will be down every week to visit."

Not me—just Jenny.

Sara felt frantic, trapped. Only children who had no one to love them and take care of them went away to school. She had Daddy and Margaret and Mrs. Dow to love her and take care of her. She couldn't go away. Not ever.

Why didn't Daddy say it was all a mistake?

"I've known Mrs. Crofton for years. The school is lovely." Margaret's voice came from a long way off. Longer away than the end of the world, where the apple tree stood in the pond.

I can't go away from here—from this house—from my friends.

Anger and rebellion surged through Sara's heart. Her hands clenched into hard fists. Her throat hurt from the effort not to cry out aloud. This was never the way she planned it. Jenny was to go away to school and then Daddy and Margaret would love Sara. Daddy and Margaret would love Sara best.

But she couldn't confess what she had done. Everyone would hate her then. No one would love her.

There was no way out.

Sara stood stiff and straight, staring at the Christmas tree.

"Let's get out the Christmas things," Margaret had said. *"We'll surprise Jenny when she comes home from school."*

And Jenny had come. She had seen Mr. Hoffman from the window of the school bus. . . .

Now all the wonder of Christmas was gone. Faded away for another year.

Sara felt a small hand touch hers, and she looked down into Jenny's tearful eyes.

Gazing up into the face of the person in the world she should least trust, Jenny said with little sobs:

"I'm glad you're going too, Sara. I don't want to go alone."

ABOUT THE AUTHOR

CAROL BEACH YORK is a full-time writer with a long list of outstanding juvenile novels to her credit, including Elsevier/Nelson's *Dead Man's Cat, Takers and Returners, I Will Make You Disappear, The Witch Lady Mystery, Beware of This Shop, Revenge of the Dolls,* and *When Midnight Comes.* Born and raised in Chicago, she sold her first story to *Seventeen* magazine. Since then, she has contributed many stories and articles to magazines in both the juvenile and adult markets, in addition to her activity as a novelist. The author lives with her daughter in Chicago.

TEENAGERS FACE LIFE AND LOVE

Choose books filled with fun and adventure, discovery and disenchantment, failure and conquest, triumph and tragedy, life and love.

☐	13359	**THE LATE GREAT ME** Sandra Scoppettone	$1.95
☐	13691	**HOME BEFORE DARK** Sue Ellen Bridgers	$1.75
☐	13671	**ALL TOGETHER NOW** Sue Ellen Bridgers	$1.95
☐	14836	**PARDON ME, YOU'RE STEPPING ON MY EYEBALL!** Paul Zindel	$2.25
☐	11091	**A HOUSE FOR JONNIE O.** Blossom Elfman	$1.95
☐	14306	**ONE FAT SUMMER** Robert Lipsyte	$1.95
☐	14690	**THE CONTENDER** Robert Lipsyte	$2.25
☐	13315	**CHLORIS AND THE WEIRDOS** Linn Platt	$1.95
☐	12577	**GENTLEHANDS** M. E. Kerr	$1.95
☐	12650	**QUEEN OF HEARTS** Bill & Vera Cleaver	$1.75
☐	12741	**MY DARLING, MY HAMBURGER** Paul Zindel	$1.95
☐	13555	**HEY DOLLFACE** Deborah Hautzig	$1.75
☐	13897	**WHERE THE RED FERN GROWS** Wilson Rawls	$2.25
☐	20170	**CONFESSIONS OF A TEENAGE BABOON** Paul Zindel	$2.25
☐	14730	**OUT OF LOVE** Hilma Wolitzer	$1.75
☐	14225	**SOMETHING FOR JOEY** Richard E. Peck	$2.25
☐	14687	**SUMMER OF MY GERMAN SOLDIER** Bette Greene	$2.25
☐	13693	**WINNING** Robin Brancato	$1.95

Buy them at your local bookstore or use this handy coupon for ordering:

Bantam Books, Inc., Dept. EDN, 414 East Golf Road, Des Plaines, Ill. 60016

Please send me the books I have checked above. I am enclosing $_____
(please add $1.00 to cover postage and handling). Send check or money order
—no cash or C.O.D.'s please.

Mr/Mrs/Miss _____

Address _____

City _____ State/Zip _____

EDN—7/81

Please allow four to six weeks for delivery. This offer expires 1/82.